PJMASKS

MONSTER OF THE DEEP!

Based on the episode "Octobella's Garden"

Simon Spotlight

New York London Toronto Sydney New Delhi

PJ Masks © 2022 FrogBox/Ent. One UK Ltd/Hasbro.
Based on the original books by Romuald *Les Pyjamasques* © 2007 first published in France by Gallimard Jeunesse.

SIMON SPOTLIGHT

An imprint of Simon & Schuster Children's Publishing Division • 1230 Avenue of the Americas, New York, New York 10020

For information about special discounts for bulk purchases, please contact Simon & Schuster Special Sales at 1-866-506-1949 or business@simonandschuster.com.
Manufactured in the United States of America 0622 LAK • 2 4 6 8 10 9 7 5 3 • ISBN 978-1-6659-1337-9 (pbk) • ISBN 978-1-6659-1338-6 (ebook)

The PJ Masks had just defeated Night Ninja one night when Armadylan arrived.

"You saved the day without me . . . again?" he asked sadly. "How can I be a hero if you never ask for my help?"

"There will be a next time," said Owlette, but Armadylan was already walking away.

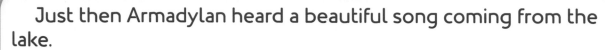

Just then Armadylan heard a beautiful song coming from the lake.

"Wow. Nice tune, tentacle girl," he told the singer.

"It's Octobella," she replied. "And thanks."

"I'm Armadylan," he said, "the strongest hero around."

Octobella giggled. "Isn't he just perfect for a squiggly little plan?" she whispered to her shrimp, Percival.

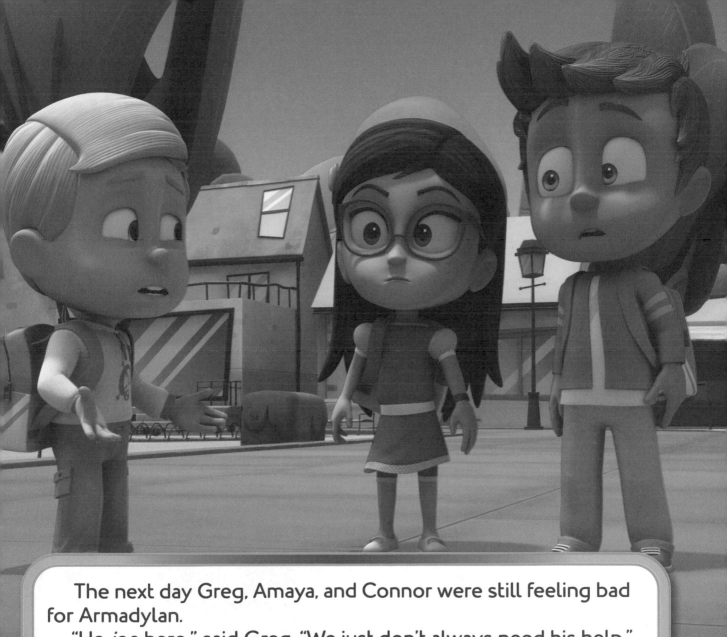

The next day Greg, Amaya, and Connor were still feeling bad for Armadylan.

"He *is* a hero," said Greg. "We just don't always need his help."

All of a sudden the trio turned a corner and saw cars overturned on the road. "What happened here?" asked Connor. "We'll check on Armadylan later. But for now . . ."

PJ MASKS, WE'RE ON OUR WAY! INTO THE NIGHT TO SAVE THE DAY.

Greg becomes Gekko!

Amaya becomes Owlette!

Connor becomes Catboy!

THEY ARE THE PJ MASKS!

On the Picture Player at HQ, the PJ Masks spotted Armadylan talking to Octobella.

"If she's up to her usual tricks, we need to warn him," said Catboy.

"What's going on with Octobella?" asked Catboy.

"We're just friends," Armadylan answered.

"You've got to be careful around her," Owlette warned.

"Yeah, she's a real monster from the deep," added Gekko.

Armadylan wasn't so sure. "You don't ask me to help with your missions, but you tell me who to be friends with?"

"We trust you. Just be careful," said Catboy. "PJ Masks, let's roll!"

Armadylan found Octobella a few minutes later. "The PJs said to stay away from you," he told her.

"So the PJs tell you what to do but never ask you to join them?" Octobella asked. "It's sad. They don't even see you as a hero."

"I'm totally a hero!" said Armadylan, easily lifting a heavy rock.

"Lucky me!" exclaimed Octobella. "I sure could use a hero's help with my underwater garden."

"I can totally do that," Armadylan offered. "But I don't have any deep-sea diving equipment."

Octobella tossed a magic bubble at Armadylan. It surrounded him and then turned into tons of bubbles! Then he began to glow green.

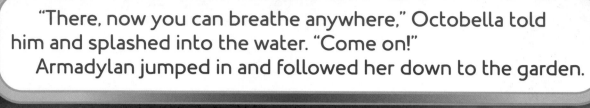

"There, now you can breathe anywhere," Octobella told him and splashed into the water. "Come on!"
Armadylan jumped in and followed her down to the garden.

Meanwhile, PJ Robot was keeping an eye on Armadylan from HQ. He sent a picture message to the PJ Masks in the Cat-Car. They saw Armadylan follow Octobella into the lake.

"Armadylan could just be on a playdate or in serious danger," said Owlette.

"With Octobella it's impossible to know," said Gekko.

It was up to the PJ Masks to find out what was going on!

A few moments later Armadylan went to Octobella's lair.
She ordered Armadylan to polish her crystals.
"A please would be nice," said Armadylan as he got to work.

The PJ Masks dove into the lake in the Gekko-Mobile. Catboy used his Cat Ears to listen in. He overheard part of Octobella's evil plan. "Octobella's going to use Armadylan for something bad," he told Gekko and Owlette.

"We need to help him!" said Gekko.

"Armadylan!" Owlette cried out.

Armadylan heard Owlette. "I wonder what the PJs are doing here," he said aloud.

"They think you can't manage on your own," said Octobella.

"I don't need them!" said Armadylan. "I'm busy helping you like a hero!"

Octobella smiled. "Well, all I need now is a special ornamental stone."

"I'll get it!" said Armadylan.

Percival led him away.

Soon the PJ Masks arrived at Octobella's garden.
"We need to find Armadylan," said Owlette.

Octobella floated above them. "Oh, your friend is long gone. I just sent him to fetch a very important crystal."
"We have to stop Armadylan from getting that crystal!" said Catboy, but Octobella blocked them from escaping her garden.

Percival led Armadylan to a stone marker. Armadylan knew just what to do.

"Underwater Thunder Thump!" he cried and smashed the stone. The crystal inside the stone floated up. He caught it and raced back to the garden.

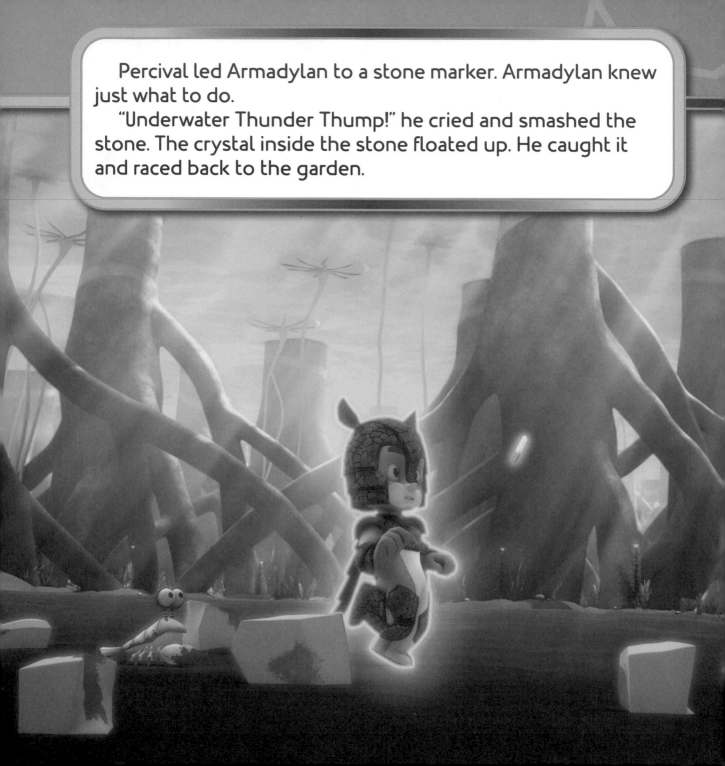

"I got it like a real hero!" Armadylan proclaimed when he saw Octobella.

"Armadylan, don't give her that stone!" cried Owlette.

"You just don't want me to help, like always," said Armadylan.

Octobella grabbed the crystal. "At last! I can finally decorate my garden . . . with PJ garden gnomes!"

Octobella pointed the crystal at the PJ Masks, and a beam of light hit them. Catboy, Owlette, and Gekko started shrinking and then got frozen in place!

Armadylan couldn't believe it. "Garden gnomes?" he asked.

"To make my garden look pretty forever," replied Octobella. "All thanks to you."

Then with a magic whirlpool, she flung Armadylan back to land . . . along with the Gekko-Mobile!

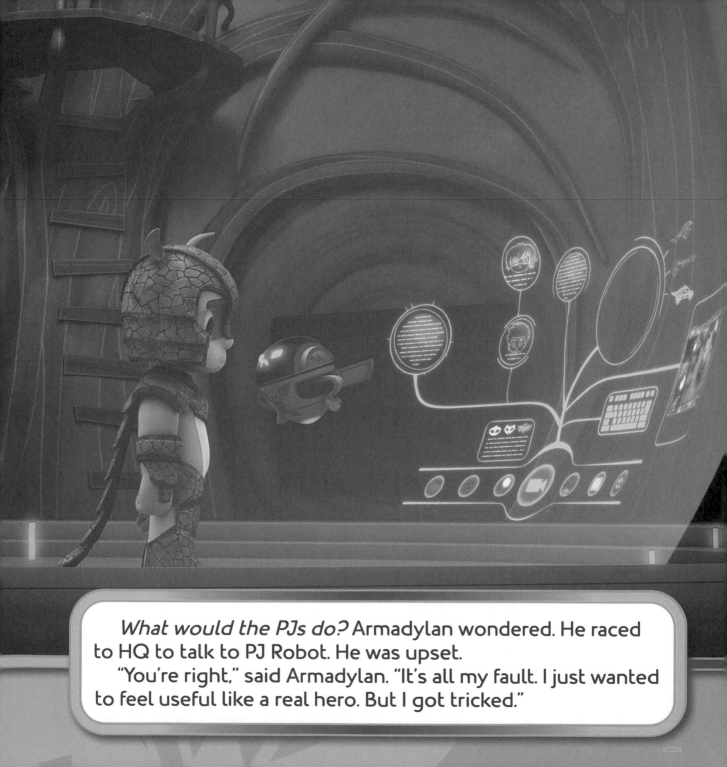

What would the PJs do? Armadylan wondered. He raced to HQ to talk to PJ Robot. He was upset.

"You're right," said Armadylan. "It's all my fault. I just wanted to feel useful like a real hero. But I got tricked."

The PJ Masks replied through the Picture Player. "Just because we don't always ask for your help—" began Owlette.

"It doesn't mean we don't think you're an awesome hero," finished Gekko.

"Sometimes we don't need help, and sometimes we do. Just so you know, right now we need it!" said Catboy.

"It's time to be heroes!" said Armadylan and PJ Robot.

Armadylan and PJ Robot drove the Gekko-Mobile back to Octobella's garden. PJ Robot snuck in and sang a song that brought the crystal to him. He used it to free the PJ Masks!

Octobella chased after them. She sang another spellbinding song! The PJ Masks and PJ Robot couldn't move! But before Octobella could bring them back to her garden, Armadylan swooped down in the Gekko-Mobile and blocked Octobella's song.

"Armadylan to the rescue!" he cried.
The heroes swam away.
"I'll get you, PJ Masks, and your friend, too!"
Octobella called after them.

Owlette smiled at Armadylan and PJ Robot. "You two totally saved us from the worst playdate ever!"

"It wasn't all bad," said Armadylan. "I got some awesome swimming practice, so I'm all set to be an underwater hero!"

"We'll definitely need you soon, underwater Armadylan," said Gekko. "But for now—"

PJ Masks all shout hooray! 'Cause in the night, we saved the day!